SEVERE WEATHER

# WILDFIRES

BY CANDICE RANSOM

WWW.APEXEDITIONS.COM



Apex is distributed by North Star Editions:
sales@northstareditions.com | 888-417-0195

Produced for Apex by Red Line Editorial.

Photographs ©: Shutterstock Images, cover, 1, 6–7, 8, 9, 12, 13, 18–19, 26–27; iStockphoto, 4–5, 10–11, 14–15, 16–17, 21, 22–23, 24–25, 27, 29

**Library of Congress Control Number: 2022901427**

**ISBN**
978-1-63738-306-3 (hardcover)
978-1-63738-342-1 (paperback)
978-1-63738-411-4 (ebook pdf)
978-1-63738-378-0 (hosted ebook)

Printed in the United States of America
Mankato, MN
082022

## NOTE TO PARENTS AND EDUCATORS

**Apex books are designed to build literacy skills in striving readers. Exciting, high-interest content attracts and holds readers' attention. The text is carefully leveled to allow students to achieve success quickly. Additional features, such as bolded glossary words for difficult terms, help build comprehension.**

# TABLE OF CONTENTS

# CHAPTER 1

# A SINGLE SPARK

It is a hot summer day. A car speeds along a road. Suddenly, its tire goes flat. A spark from the tire skips to the dry grass. It starts a fire.

Many wildfires start small. But they spread very fast.

The fire spreads quickly to nearby trees. The crackling blaze grows hotter. Soon, the whole forest is burning.

Some wildfires can travel 14 miles per hour (23 km/h).

**FAST FACT**

Some wildfires can start from just the heat of the sun.

Smoke rises into the air. The sky turns dark orange. The fire lasts for days. Finally, firefighters get it under control.

**Wildfires may be called forest fires or brush fires, depending on what they burn.**

By clearing the ground, fires can help new plants have space and sunlight.

## GOOD AND BAD

Wildfires can be harmful. They damage land and buildings. And their smoke pollutes the air. But not all wildfires are bad. Some kill dead trees. Then new, healthy trees can grow.

CHAPTER 2

# A BIG BURN

A wildfire is a large fire that spreads quickly. Some wildfires start when lightning strikes. But most are caused by people.

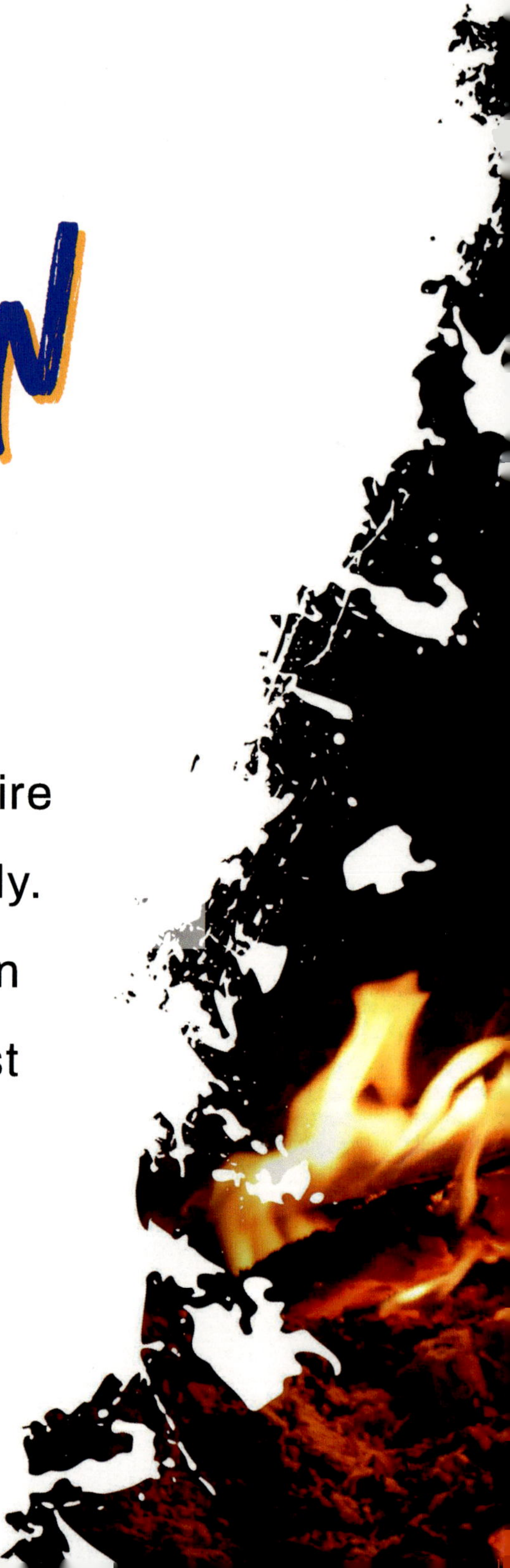

Humans can cause wildfires by leaving campfires unwatched.

Smoke and sparks from wildfires can rise high into the air.

Like all fires, wildfires need heat, **fuel**, and **oxygen**. Wind helps fires grow. It spreads flames to new areas.

If wildfires get near people's homes, people must leave right away.

## FAST FACT

Humans cause about 90 percent of wildfires.

Wildfires happen all around the world. They are most common in places with lots of plants and little rain. Many wildfires take place during the summer. Hot weather can help fires spread.

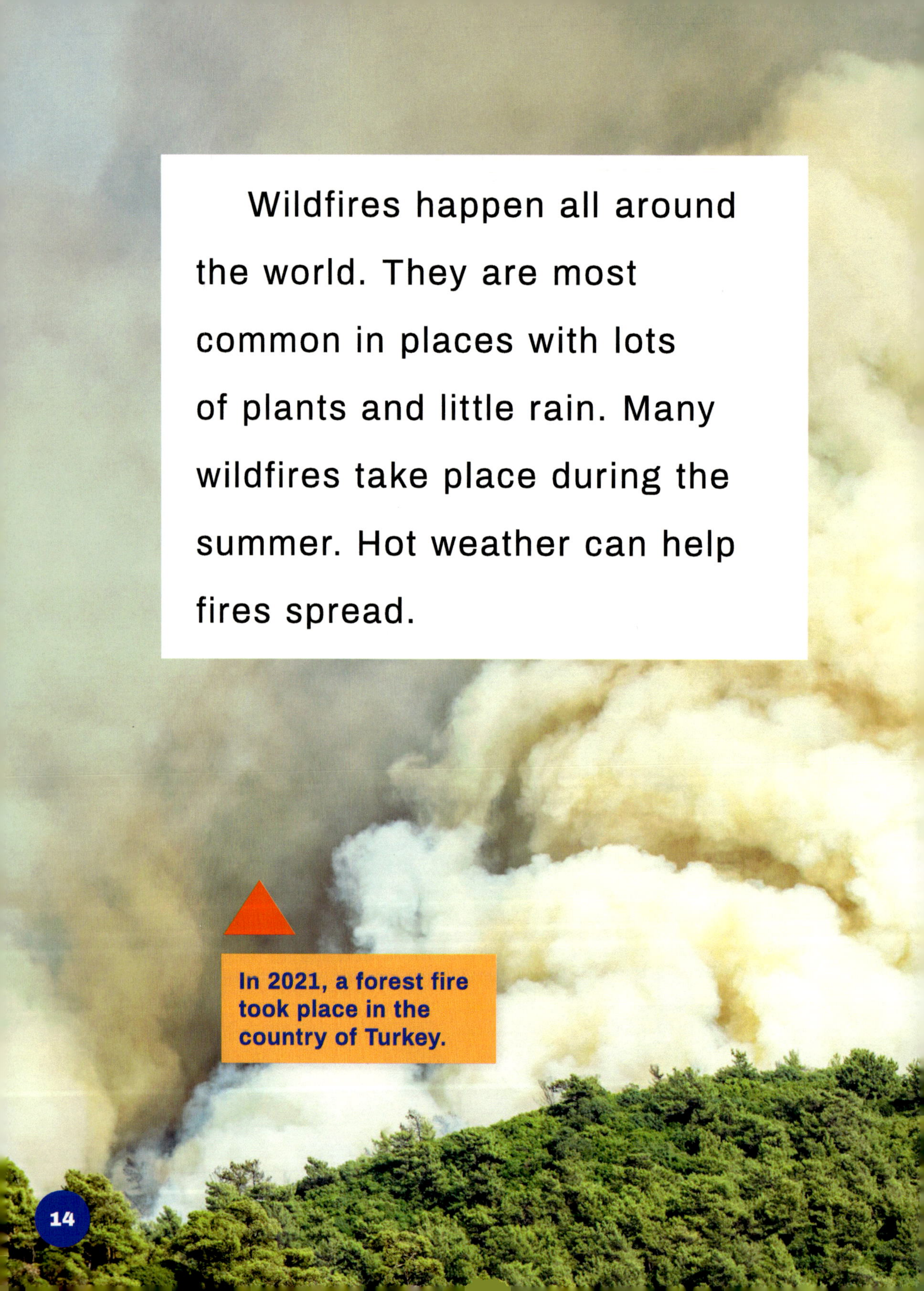

In 2021, a forest fire took place in the country of Turkey.

# WORSE WILDFIRES

**Climate change** has brought warmer air everywhere. **Droughts** are getting worse. Plants are drying out. As a result, wildfires can start more easily. They spread faster, too.

CHAPTER 3

# FAMOUS FIRES

Wildfires can be very dangerous. One huge fire scorched Wisconsin and Michigan in 1871. The fire burned several cities. Many people died.

The Great Peshtigo Fire of 1871 was the deadliest forest fire in US history.

In 2011, Texas had many wildfires because of a bad drought.

In 2011, Texas had more than 30,000 wildfires. They burned nearly four million **acres** (2 million ha) of land. Thousands of people lost their homes.

**FAST FACT**

Fires that burn more than 100,000 acres (40,000 ha) are called megafires.

In 2019 and 2020, wildfires burned 46 million acres (19 million ha) in Australia. Smoke and ash filled the air. The fires caused problems in places many miles away.

## FIRE IN PARADISE

**California has many dangerous wildfires. One fast-moving fire swept through the town of Paradise in 2018. It killed 85 people. More than 18,000 buildings were destroyed.**



**Wildfires in Australia destroyed the homes of both people and animals.**

CHAPTER 4

# FIGHTING FIRES

Wildfires are hard to control. But people have ways to stop them. Some people make **firebreaks**. Firebreaks clear away trees and plants. Without fuel, fire can't spread.

A firebreak can help slow the spread of a wildfire.

Controlled burns also help. Firefighters start fires on purpose. These fires remove grass or plants. They stop other fires from getting out of control.

Firefighters watch controlled burns carefully to make sure the fires don't get too big.

## FAST FACT

People place cameras in some forests to watch for fires.

Scientists use **satellites** to track wildfires. They can warn people near the fire. Then they can send firefighters to put the fire out.

Satellites can take photos of wildfires from space.

Some firefighters fly helicopters. They dump water on wildfires.

## TYPES OF FIREFIGHTERS

Many firefighters help stop wildfires. Some spray water and foam at the fires. Smoke jumpers leap from planes to reach the flames. Other teams fight the most dangerous blazes.

# COMPREHENSION QUESTIONS

*Write your answers on a separate piece of paper.*

**1.** Write a few sentences describing how wildfires form.

**2.** Would you want to be a smoke jumper? Why or why not?

**3.** What three things do wildfires need to burn?

- **A.** heat, fuel, and oxygen
- **B.** fuel, air, and water
- **C.** trees, sparks, and grass

**4.** Why do scientists warn people about nearby wildfires?

- **A.** so people can help the fires spread
- **B.** so people can go closer to the fires
- **C.** so people have time to get away

**5.** What does **scorched** mean in this book?

***One huge fire scorched Wisconsin and Michigan in 1871. The fire burned several cities.***

**A.** helped
**B.** burned badly
**C.** stayed away

**6.** What does **controlled** mean in this book?

***Controlled burns also help. Firefighters start fires on purpose.***

**A.** done by mistake
**B.** wild and free
**C.** limited and planned

*Answer key on page 32.*

# GLOSSARY

**acres**

Units for measuring land. One acre is about the size of a football field.

**climate change**

A dangerous long-term change in Earth's temperature and weather patterns.

**droughts**

Times of little or no rain.

**firebreaks**

Strips of land cleared of bushes and trees.

**fuel**

Material, such as wood, that can burn and release heat.

**oxygen**

A gas in the air. Animals need oxygen to breathe, and fires need it to burn.

**pollutes**

Makes something dirty or unsafe.

**satellites**

Spacecraft that orbit Earth, often to collect information.

# TO LEARN MORE

## BOOKS

London, Martha. *Wildfires*. Minneapolis: Abdo Publishing, 2020.

Maurer, Tracy Nelson. *The World's Worst Wildfires*. North Mankato, MN: Capstone Press, 2019.

Potenza, Alessandra. *All About Wildfires*. New York: Scholastic, 2021.

## ONLINE RESOURCES

Visit **www.apexeditions.com** to find links and resources related to this title.

## ABOUT THE AUTHOR

Candice Ransom is the author of 165 books for children. Fifty of those books are nonfiction. She loves to learn something new, whether it's about dinosaurs, rocks, or weather. She lives with her husband and two cats in Fredericksburg, Virginia.

# INDEX



**ANSWER KEY:**
1. Answers will vary; 2. Answers will vary; 3. A; 4. C; 5. B; 6. C